A Whiff of Danger

Other Avon Camelot Books by
Nancy Hope Wilson

NANCY HOPE WILSON was born in Boston and grew up in suburban Massachusetts and rural Vermont. She is a graduate of Swarthmore College and the Harvard Graduate School of Education, and she has taught in day care centers, elementary schools, high schools, nursing homes, and human service agencies. She also worked for five years as a carpenter. Her other books include three novels, *Bringing Nettie Back, The Reason for Janey,* and *A Nose for Trouble,* and a picture book, *Helen and the Hudson Hornet.* She lives in Amherst, Massachusetts, with her husband and two children.

A Whiff of Danger

NANCY HOPE WILSON

Illustrated by Marie DeJohn

AN AVON CAMELOT BOOK

A WHIFF OF DANGER is an original publication of Avon Books. This work
has never before appeared in book form.

AVON BOOKS
A division of
The Hearst Corporation
1350 Avenue of the Americas
New York, New York 10019

Copyright © 1996 by Nancy Hope Wilson
Illustrations copyright © 1996 by Avon Books
Illustrations by Marie DeJohn
Published by arrangement with the author
Library of Congress Catalog Card Number: 95-94264
ISBN: 0-380-78276-6
RL: 4.9

First Avon Camelot Printing: September 1996

CAMELOT TRADEMARK REG. U.S. PAT. OFF. AND IN OTHER COUNTRIES, MARCA REGIS-
TRADA, HECHO EN U.S.A.

Printed in the U.S.A.

OPM   10   9   8   7   6   5   4   3   2   1

To Andrea, Evan, and the original Maggie May, with love

ACKNOWLEDGMENTS

Thanks to Paul Markoski and Allan LaPointe of the Berkshire Gas Company for not thinking I was nuts when I walked up to their truck and started asking them questions. Thanks to my daughter, Hannah Jenckes Simms, for drawing the map. Thanks, as always, to my critique group for their wise and supportive suggestions. And thanks to Anne Dunn for hers.

A Whiff of Danger

ONE

"Quiet!" Mr. Buckley commanded.

He was erasing the blackboard, making my nose tickle from chalk dust. He hadn't mentioned Halloween all day, but his tie had black and orange stripes.

"No homework tonight," he announced. "I expect you'll be otherwise engaged."

Everyone started talking again. At the back table, Mark Lowman and his buddies were making a big show of whispering and snickering. Mark's the kind of kid who probably drapes trees with toilet paper on Halloween.

On my first day at Lansford Elementary, Mark acted like a jerk about my wheelchair. Then I beat him at arm wrestling. He'd promised in front of everyone to quit the put-downs if I won, but he still acts like he has something to prove.

"On second thought," Mr. Buckley announced, "I *do* have an assignment for you." We all groaned. "Stay out of trouble," he said. The noise picked up again. "AND . . ." We all looked at him. "Stay out of danger." Then he smiled, but he still didn't mention Halloween.

We were all putting away our math work and getting ready to leave. I twisted around to close up the saddlebag at the back of my wheelchair. Suddenly I could smell licorice— Halloween jelly beans, I figured. I have a very sensitive nose. Some people call it a nose for trouble, but there are just as many good smells as bad ones.

Debby leaned over from the next table.

"Hey Maggie," she whispered, and I knew who had the jelly beans.

"Got any orange ones left?" I asked.

"Huh?"

"Jelly beans," I said. "The orange are my favorite."

"Oh sure," Deb said, and dug into her backpack. "But I was trying to tell you: A bunch of us are going over to Jo's tonight." She gave me some jelly beans. "You want to come? Tina and I—"

I saw Jo give Debby's braid a sharp tug.

"Ow!" Debby said. "What the . . . ?"

"That's okay," I said quickly. "I'm taking my little brother out anyway."

Debby always forgets things like my needing a ramp wherever I go. Jo's always quick to remind her.

"But thanks, Deb," I said.

"You have a little brother?" Jo asked. Jo and Deb and Tina hang out together. They've been really friendly from the start, but somehow in two whole months of fifth grade, Jo hasn't learned much about me.

3

"Oh come on, Jo," Tina said. "Don't you know *that*? Her brother's name is Howie. He's four, right Maggie?" Tina and I have had some real talks.

"Yeah," I said. "He's going as the cowardly lion—you know, from *The Wizard of Oz*. He wants me to be the tin man."

"Quiet!" Mr. Buckley said again.

I turned back to my table. Mr. Buckley doesn't have desks or assigned seats, but after the first week, we all just seemed to keep the same places. I sit next to Cedrick Zinger. He's new, too, but supershy. I'm the only friend he's made so far. If people call him Cedrick, he corrects them: "Just Rick," he says. So I got to calling him Just Rick. He was scribbling a note to me.

"Need a scarecrow?" it said.

"Yeah," I wrote back. Then I added, "But the scarecrow had no brain." Just Rick's the brainiest kid I've ever met.

He scribbled right back, "Well the tin man had no heart."

I grinned at him, but he started turning

4

pink, so I just wrote, "5:30. 42 Greene Street. Be there."

"I repeat," Mr. Buckley was saying, "*walkers*, please line up." He was looking straight at Just Rick, who turned bright red and jumped up so fast, he bumped smack into Mark Lowman.

"Hey watch it, you wim—!" Mark cut himself short, but he scowled—as if the smallest kid in the class could be a threat to Macho Man. I don't know what Mark's got against Just Rick. Maybe it's that Rick's smart, or maybe it's that he's so shy; probably it's that he's my friend.

Mark elbowed into the walkers' line in front of Just Rick.

"Bus one," Mr. Buckley called out. I wheeled over toward the door. I don't go on bus one, of course. I have to go on a special van even though I live pretty near the school. But Mr. Buckley never singled me out. He just started looking at me when he called the first bus. Mr. Buckley and I get along.

As the walkers filed out, I saw Mark Lowman bend to pick up some paper from the floor. It surprised me that he'd bother, but I was talking to Tina and didn't stop to think much about it. It did occur to me, though, that a kid who stoops to pick up trash might not be a *total* jerk.

TWO

My mom gets a little goofy on Halloween.

Last year she wore a tea cozy on her head. It's a cushiony thing she puts over her teapot to keep it hot. She answered the door with that on her head and a white dust mask over her nose and mouth—the kind Dad uses for carpentry. That was in our old neighborhood, where I was already used to being different.

"Hey, Mom," I asked at supper, "what's your costume this year?"

"Don't know yet," she said, which was probably true. She always makes up something at the last minute.

Dad chuckled. "I can hardly wait."

Howie was too excited to eat. There were already kids out making the rounds. Every time the doorbell rang, Howie jumped up to answer it.

"*I'm* going to be the cowardly lion," he announced to everyone. "Can I get dressed now, Mom?"

While Mom helped Howie into his ears and mane and whiskers and tail, Dad helped me wrap my arms and legs in tinfoil. We used a lot of silver duct tape. My hair's really blond, so Mom gave me a gray knee-stocking to cover it.

"I'll get a funnel," Dad said.

Meanwhile, I smeared gray greasepaint on my face. Greasepaint is the kind of thing Mom keeps on hand. It smelled wonderful— like crayons, but more oily and sharp. It made me remember the play I'd done in fourth grade. That's what I mean about good smells. Suddenly my mind was back in my old school with all my old friends.

Then I realized Dad was standing there, holding a big funnel from the garage.

"Thanks," I said, but I guess my nose wrinkled. Even over the greasepaint, I could smell gasoline.

Dad laughed. "I already scrubbed it."

"Maybe I'll scrub it some more," I said.

Dad leaned over to hug me. "That's my Maggie May Mitzkovitz! Always *nose* what she wants!"

"Ha ha," I said, "very punny. And now you've got greasepaint on your cheek!"

Dad went into the kitchen to find a paper towel.

Then I heard a big roar from the next room. Howie appeared, making claws with his hands. He roared some more.

I went all stiff in my chair. "Ol cn," I squeaked, not even moving my eyes. "Ol cn."

"Oil can!" Howie yelled, and pretended to oil my chair.

The doorbell rang again.

Howie ran to answer it and this time I followed. It was 5:30. Knowing Just Rick, he'd be right on time.

"It's the scarecrow!" Howie said.

Being a little scrawny came naturally to Just Rick, but he'd also found a straw hat and floppy clothes. He'd stuck broom straw in his sleeves, but his shirt was stuffed with dry leaves. As he rustled through the door, a few of them fluttered to the floor.

I scooped them up and crushed them near my nose. They didn't smell right—more like burned toast. "Oof!" I said. "This grease-paint changes everything!"

Just Rick looked at his feet. "Sorry I'm late," he said. "My dog tried to follow me."

I laughed. "You're not late."

But then Howie screamed and started flapping his hands the way he does when he's really scared. "A witch, Maggie, a *real* one!'' He was pointing outside and climbing into my lap all at once.

I looked beyond the ramp toward the sidewalk. There *was* a witch there, and she did look awfully real. She was in a long black cape and her hair was all wild and scraggly. She wasn't wearing a hat, but even from a distance, I could see her sharp nose and deep eyes.

''Close the door!'' Howie screamed, and Just Rick did.

''It's okay, Howie,'' I said. ''It's just a mask. You wait and see. When she rings the bell, I'll get her to take it off. Okay?''

Howie got down from my lap. ''Maybe it's the witch from the haunted house.''

''Oh come on, Howser,'' I said. There actually is a huge old house on our street, but Mom says old Mrs. Greene lives there. I ruffled Howie's mane. ''There aren't any real witches,'' I said. ''Now where's your courage, Mr. Lion?''

Howie roared at Just Rick, who jumped back and cowered.

That's when Mom came down the stairs. I couldn't believe it. She was in her same sweatshirt and sweatpants, but there were round blue stickers all over her—on her clothes, on her hands, in her hair, on her face.

"How do I look?" she asked me. "I found these in my desk." She twirled once, then put out her hand to Just Rick. She glanced at me to remind me of my manners.

"Uh, this is my mom," I said. "Mom, this is Just Rick—no, I mean just—*Rick* Zinger."

"Pleased to meet you, Rick," Mom said.

Just Rick put out his hand to Mom, but he had his head down. He was looking away. I knew he was shy, but this was embarrassing. Then I realized his shoulders were shaking. Suddenly he took in a deep, snorting breath. He was laughing! I'd never seen Just Rick laugh, and it made me grin.

"What's so funny?" I asked. Dad was just coming back from the kitchen.

"Sorry," Just Rick said. He tried to

straighten his face. "But I think your mom's gone dotty!" Then he really laughed, because Mom and Dad had joined him.

I didn't get it, but I laughed along for the ride.

"What's so funny?" Howie asked, and Dad explained about *dotty* meaning crazy. Just Rick probably knows every word in the dictionary.

"Can we go now?" Howie asked.

Mom and Dad wanted to remind us one last time about our route, as if I didn't already have it memorized. They're nervous about not knowing all the neighbors yet.

"Don't worry," I said. "I made us a map. Where'd you put it, Howser?"

He dug it out of his trick-or-treat bag, and unfolded it for Mom and Dad. We were going in a big L—up Greene Street and back, and then to the end of Greene Lane and back. The big house was on the inside corner, but it was off-limits. We'd never even seen Mrs. Greene. Given how weird her house was, I wasn't sure I wanted to.

Howie held up both hands with the fingers spread out. "Ten!" he said. "Ten houses. Ten candies!" His tail bounced as he jumped up and down. "*Now* can we go?"

But as Dad opened the door to usher us out, Howie actually held back for a second. "Is the witch gone?" he asked.

That's the only reason I noticed she'd never shown up at the door.

THREE

I paused for a minute at the top of the ramp. It was a perfect fall night—fresh and crisp, but not cold. I could see little groups of kids crossing under the streetlights or standing on the neighbors' porches while their parents waited in the shadows. It wasn't so different from my old neighborhood.

We'd set our four jack-o-lanterns in a line

down the ramp. I took a deep breath to get that great scorched-pumpkin smell, but instead, I smelled something like a dirty gerbil cage.

"I hate this," I said, and Just Rick looked back up the ramp at me. "Between my face paint and this gas funnel," I explained, "it's like my head's in a box. Smells get all messed up."

"Masked," Just Rick said as I rolled down the ramp.

"Huh?"

"That's what it's called—one smell masks another."

"So my disguise is disguising smells?"

Just Rick just smiled. He was leaning over into the pumpkin light to push the candle flames away from the wooden rail. There wasn't any danger, but the Zingers moved here after their house burned down. Rick gets very nervous about fire.

"Thanks," I said.

"Hurry up!" Howie called.

He'd started up the sidewalk, but had stopped to wait for us, and I knew why: He was eyeing Mrs. Greene's house across the street. Even in the daytime, that place is pretty spooky. It's dark grey and huge, with towers like an old castle. Dad calls it Victorian. He says the whole neighborhood was built on land that used to belong to Mrs. Greene. He heard the house still has gaslight fixtures on the walls and a real icebox with a compartment for a huge block of ice. Being a builder, Dad gets excited about houses.

What *I* wonder about that place is: Why are all the shades pulled down day and night?

When we caught up to Howie, he pointed at the big house. "That's where the witch lives," he announced to Just Rick.

"Oh, come off it, Howser," I said, but the house did give me the creeps. It was so dark, it made the sky look pale.

"Which way?" Howie asked, as if that were why he'd stopped.

"Well, you *could* go that way," Just Rick said in a goofy voice. He flopped his arms around, pointing every which way like the scarecrow. "Or that way. Or some people do go both ways."

Howie giggled and ran on ahead of us again.

I was just getting my wheels rolling again when I stopped short. "Hey, what's that smell?"

I tried to catch another whiff. I wasn't even sure I'd smelled anything, but something had made me think, *Danger!*

Just Rick patted his rustly shirt. "All I can smell is dried leaves."

"And all *I* can smell is this stupid greasepaint!"

"Hurry up!" Howie called from the steps of the Woynars' house.

At the Woynars, I could roll right up to the bottom of the steps.

"Trick or treat!" Howie roared when the

door opened. "Give me some candy or I'll eat you up."

Mr. Woynar backed away. "Hey! I thought you were supposed to be cowardly." He reached out to drop a candy bar into Howie's bag.

"I think candy gives him courage," I said.

Mr. Woynar chuckled. He handed Just Rick a candy bar and tossed one to me.

"Thanks!" we all called, already on our way.

At the Hickmans', I had to wait on the sidewalk, because of a pile of leaves across the walk. The leaves were already rotting. I usually like that damp smell, but combined with greasepaint and gasoline, it reminded me of moldy potatoes. I was waiting there wishing Mrs. Hickman would quit admiring Howie's costume, when I saw something move in the Hickmans' backyard. I peered into the darkness: Nothing. I'd been imagining things. I was about to look away, when my eye caught an odd shape. I could just make out the outline of a wild-haired figure standing motionless under a tree.

All I could think about was the big house and Mrs. Greene. What if that awful face *wasn't* a mask?

FOUR

I moved my chair back and forth until I could reach down with my funnel and shove some of the leaves out of the way. I had to back up again to get a head start, but on the second try I got over the bump of leaves. I sped up the walk into the light.

Just Rick and Howie were coming down the steps.

I made myself smile. I was already feeling silly for being scared, but my heart was still pounding.

"Look, Mags!" Howie said. "Red licorice! Can I have it now?"

"Sure," I said. If he saw that witch, he'd need all the courage he could get. "Did you get me some?" I asked. I tried not to sound out of breath.

Rick handed me my candy. "Are you okay?" he asked, but I couldn't exactly explain in front of Howie.

I decided not to eat my red licorice. I'd just opened Howie's for him, and it smelled like Mom's plant fertilizer.

All this time, we'd been stopped there in the middle of the Hickmans' walk. Two kids in monster costumes passed us. They were pretty tame, but Howie still sort of hid behind my chair.

"Look," I said to him. "Let's go to Steffie's next."

Steffie's house was back the other way, across the street from ours. I wanted to give that witch some time to get lost.

"But, Maggie," Howie said. He pulled out the crumpled map and held it up to the light.

"I know," I said. "We've still got some houses up this way, but—"

"Three," Howie said, and held up three fingers.

The two monsters stared at us as they left.

"Yeah," I said to Howie, "but—well—I just remembered—Steffie said to go there early. You know—in case she runs out of candy."

"Oh! Let's go!"

Howie checked to be sure the monsters had turned the other way, then skipped out ahead of us.

I asked Just Rick to give me a push over the leaves. He leaned down near my ear. "What's up?"

"W-i-t-c-h," I spelled.

Howie turned around. "What's *that* spell?" He's been trying to spell words recently. I'd only attracted his attention.

"It spells . . ." I drew the word out so I could think a second. "It spells . . . Beat you to our house!" I said, and pushed my wheelchair into high speed.

26

It worked. Howie giggled and ran after me until I let him get ahead. His mane flopped and his tail bounced and he didn't even glance across the street when we passed the big house.

I did, though.

Howie stopped on the sidewalk in front of our house. "I won!" he yelled as I caught up. "I won!"

We both waited there for Just Rick, who had slowed to a walk. I've already noticed at school that he's not exactly an athlete.

Howie was hopping from one foot to the other.

"Do you need to go to the bathroom?" I asked.

He stopped still and thought for a second. "Yeah." Suddenly it seemed urgent, and he ran up the walk and up the ramp.

Mom was just opening our door to a cowboy and a bumble bee. I think they backed away a little when they saw the blue dots. Howie dashed in past Mom, and I saw her

27

laugh as she handed out candy. Then she waved at me before she closed the door.

Now I could talk to Just Rick.

"That witch," I said. "She isn't trick-or-treating. At that last house, she was hiding out back."

"She's only some kid, Maggie!"

"How do *you* know? Have *you* ever seen Mrs. Greene?"

Just Rick smiled. "You're spooked, aren't you?"

I didn't answer. I just sat up straighter and adjusted my funnel hat. "You don't scare easy, do you?" I said to Just Rick.

"Depends," he said.

"Oh yeah."

After what happened on the first day of school, *everyone* knows Rick's scared of fire. Not just scared—terrified. *So* terrified that he does crazy, brave things. When the fire alarm kept going off that day, and he thought I was trapped in the school, he went in after me. I was fine, but *he* nearly fainted from fear. Finally, I smelled hot wires, and the fire chief found a short circuit. He acted like I was a hero, but Rick was the one who'd been brave.

"Here comes Howie," I said. "All set, Howser?"

"Yeah. Come on! Steffie might run out!"

Steffie's house is on the other corner of Greene Street and Greene Lane, which means our house faces the side of hers, and her house faces the side of Mrs. Greene's. We know Steffie best of any of our neighbors, because even though she's old and stiff, she's always out in her flower gardens, weeding and watering, watering and weeding.

Howie ran right up onto the porch and rang the bell. I stopped halfway up the walk because there was a huge coil of garden hose in the way. Rick tried to move it, but he couldn't lift the whole pile. He started to uncoil it.

"That's okay," I said. "But don't forget my candy."

Just Rick grinned at me. "Unless she's run out," he said.

Steffie moves kind of slowly, so we had to

wait a minute for her to answer the bell. Here I was, stuck by myself again outside the light. I faced my chair squarely toward Steffie's door. I was determined not to look at the big house. But just thinking about it made my back tingle. What if that stupid witch was creeping up on me? I turned my chair around fast and looked across the lane. I could see the side of the big house. I could see the back porch and the big overgrown backyard that was fenced off from the neighbors but not from the road. Two kids and a parent were walking down that side of the lane. I tried to figure out the kids' costumes—a king and a queen, maybe? It had to be my imagination that something moved beyond them—on Mrs. Greene's back porch.

Suddenly, Steffie answered the door, all smiles and chatter and excitement. When she saw me, she made a point of coming down the walk and handing me my candy. Even my greasepaint couldn't disguise the smell of her rose perfume.

When we left Steffie's and headed up the

lane, I didn't say a word about what I'd seen. I'd only scare Howie and show Rick how spooked I was. Even when I caught a whiff of something nasty again, I didn't say a thing. Maybe it was Steffie's chrysanthemums masked by my stupid disguise.

By the time we'd gone to the houses up the lane and around the little circle at the end, I was having fun again. Outside of school, Just Rick was turning out to be—I don't know—*silly*. He flopped his arms around and tried to kick up his heels. Once, he fell down and lost half his leaves. Howie and I were both laughing when we passed alongside the big house again.

Even when I thought I saw someone on that back porch again, I refused to say a thing.

Then the witch lit a match.

It was only a match, but the way it burst into the darkness, it seemed like a huge explosion. I heard Just Rick gasp, and Howie stood there for a frozen second before he started flapping his free hand. His mouth was wide open, but I guess he was too scared to scream.

The witch held the match under her chin, making her face look all shadowy. I suddenly felt sick to my stomach. I rolled right up to Howie and pulled him into my lap.

"Cut it out!" I hollered at the witch.

She cackled and called in a high, squeaky voice, "Want to play with fire, scarecrow?"

This had to be somebody's stupid idea of a joke. Right?

I glanced at Just Rick, half thinking he might be part of it. No way. He looked as scared as Howie.

With Howie still on my lap, I maneuvered my chair to grab Just Rick by the elbow. I didn't want him doing anything brave.

The match had gone out. I even got a whiff of the smoke. Was that the danger I'd been catching on the wind?

"Come on," I said. "Let's get out of here."

"That old house would go up like tinder," Rick muttered. We were crossing back over Greene Street. "Maybe we should call the fire department."

Now that the witch was out of sight, Howie perked up a little. "Fire trucks?" he said.

I was still trying to calm myself down. "Cut it out, you guys. It was only a match. You want to go home now, Howser?"

Howie scrambled off my lap. "Remember?" he said. He stuck up three fingers. Maybe candy really did give him courage.

"Okay," I said. I looked at Just Rick. He shrugged and actually smiled.

Then Dad called from our doorway. "Hey, Maggie! Kids! Come here quick!"

FIVE

"What?" I called back to Dad.

He just beckoned.

"We're not finished!" Howie said, and put up three fingers.

"Come here," Dad said.

When I got to the bottom of the ramp, I asked him again what was up, but he was being mysterious. From the hint of a smile in his voice, I figured Mom had added something new and creative to her costume, but why couldn't it wait?

When I got inside the door, Mom was coming out of the kitchen with a big grin on her blue-dotted face. Her costume hadn't changed, except that some of the stickers were starting to peel off.

Then I saw someone right behind her. Someone familiar but totally unexpected.

"Tina!"

"Hi," Tina said. She was smiling at my surprise. "Hi, Rick," she said. She didn't wait for us to ask. "I was at Jo's party," she explained, "but it turned out her parents weren't there, and her sister *was* there." Jo has a sister in high school. "And a whole bunch of her sisters' friends showed up, and . . ." She glanced at Mom and Dad. "It wasn't my kind of scene."

"But her folks are out," Dad said, "so she called here, and I went and got her." Dad hadn't even met Tina before, but he acted proud of her.

Mom laughed. "So now, Maggie, *all* your friends think your mom's nuts."

Tina smiled. "Definitely a little different."

36

Howie walked over to Tina and looked her up and down. "You have braids," he said. "You can be Dorothy."

Tina laughed. She has braids all over her head. "You must be Howie," she said. "Or rather—the cowardly lion."

Howie roared at her. "We already saw the wicked witch," he said. "The *real* one!"

I glanced at Just Rick, but Mom and Dad were just smiling as Howie went on.

"And she tried to scare the scarecrow with fire, and I got scared, too, but then I got brave."

Tina laughed again. "Yeah, I know the story."

Mom went into the kitchen and came back with a basket. "Here, Dorothy," she said. "Sorry we don't have ruby slippers."

"What's that smell?" I asked.

"You and your nose," Mom said. "There were onions in that basket."

"Onions?" I said. It smelled more like dirty socks. It made me nervous, not being able to trust my nose.

"Well," Dad said. "Follow the yellow brick road!"

He opened the door for us.

In waddled a basset hound.

"Zelda!" Just Rick said. "I told you to stay home!" He was trying to sound stern, but the dog put her paws up on him and whined. He crouched down to pet her and let her lick his face. "Aw, Zellie. How'd you find me?" So much for sternness.

"She can be Toto," Howie announced, and went out the door.

Mom and Dad thought *that* was funny too, but I was getting a little spooked again. It was *too* much like the story. I was half afraid that when we got outside, there'd be a swarm of flying monkeys.

Instead, there was a swarm of kids: some clowns, some superheroes, a rabbit, and a box of Cheerios. I had to laugh at myself.

"Great costume," I said as I passed the Cheerios.

We headed up Greene Street again, with Howie and Zelda in the lead.

"So," I said to Tina. "What was happening at Jo's?"

"Wow, Maggie," Just Rick said. "Even *I* can smell cigarettes!"

"Jo was *smoking*?" I said. Maybe that was the dirty-socks smell.

"Not Jo," Tina said. "Jo's not dumb. Her sister and those friends."

"A cigarette," Just Rick said, "is what started the fire."

We didn't have to ask what fire.

"Your parents smoke?" All I'd ever smelled on Just Rick was toothpaste or shampoo.

"The guy downstairs," he said. "It was a two-family."

It was the most he'd ever told me about the fire. I wheeled along in silence for a while, in case he wanted to say more.

"Some house!" Tina commented as we passed Mrs. Greene's.

I didn't look across the street. I watched Howie and Zelda. Their tails were wagging in unison.

40

"Zelda's the one who woke us up," Just Rick said.

No wonder he couldn't be stern with her.

Then Zelda barked and Howie screamed. He was flapping the hand that wasn't pointing across the street. I caught up to Howie fast. It was the witch again, of course. She was standing in the side yard of the big house.

Suddenly, I didn't feel spooked at all. I just felt *very* angry.

"Get lost!" I hollered at the witch. "You old hag!"

I hugged Howie as she cackled and lit another match.

Zelda barked again and took off across the street.

"No, Zelda!" Just Rick called, but clearly obedience wasn't Zelda's main event.

The witch turned and ran into the high, dry grass. Zelda ran after her. Just Rick ran after Zelda.

All I could do was sit there and watch, holding Howie safe.

Within a few seconds, the witch and Zelda and Rick had all disappeared into the darkness. We heard Zelda barking. We heard Just Rick calling her. We heard a long, nasty cackle. Then we heard nothing at all.

SIX

For a minute, Tina and Howie and I were sort of stuck there. We stared across the street as if there were something to see. That big group of trick-or-treaters passed us and slowed down to gape. I couldn't blame them. There I was with my funnel hat all cockeyed and a lion still cowering in my lap. Tina had dropped her basket.

Finally, she bent to pick it up. "What now?" she said.

Howie got off my lap. I still sat there for a second, filling up with anger. When I was full to bursting, I turned my chair around.

"All I know," I said, "is now I'm going to *catch* that stupid witch." I didn't care if she was real or not.

"But how do we do that?" Tina asked.

I smiled at her. "We?"

Tina smiled back.

I had to think for a minute. I sure couldn't chase anyone into that overgrown grass. And if Tina went after Just Rick, I might lose her, too.

"Look," I said. "There's a big fence on two sides of that yard. They'll have to come back this way or end up on the lane."

"Lane?"

"Around the corner."

"You want me to wait here?" Tina asked.

"You don't mind?"

She shrugged. " 'Course not."

"Great. If Rick comes back this way, holler, okay?"

44

"Sure," Tina said. She didn't seem scared at all.

Howie was still staying close. I couldn't hold his hand and move fast. Pushing one-sided makes my chair wobble. I thought of taking him home, but then Mom and Dad might call us all in. I clenched my teeth. I absolutely *couldn't* let that witch get away with this.

"Hey, King of the Forest," I said, "got any courage left?"

Howie peered into the depths of his candy bag. "Lots," he said. He even smiled a little.

"Let me see."

He held the open bag up to my face.

"Wow!" I said. Then I frowned. "But does that stuff really work?"

He reached his whole arm into the bag and brought out a miniature coconut candy bar. "This kind does!"

"I don't know," I said, shaking my head. "That doesn't look strong enough."

Howie'd already ripped off the wrapper.

45

"Sure it is!" He stuffed the whole candy into his mouth. "Schee?" he said with his mouth still full. (*Now* I smelled something like onions.) Howie stood a little taller already. "Schee? It's weal schtrongh, Magsch!" Then he swallowed. "Strong enough for what?"

"The scarecrow's gone after the witch," I said. "The tin man and the lion have to help."

"Oh."

Howie reached for another candy.

I got him to go with me around the corner. He even stuck by me when I went up the dark side of the lane, near the big house. That way I could see and not be seen. Howie held on to a back handle of my chair, but otherwise, he really was brave.

I was the one having second thoughts. My stomach even felt uneasy again. I kept getting whiffs of that danger smell. I wished I could trust my nose. What was I doing here anyway? And where were Rick and Zelda?

Then I heard rustling noises on Mrs. Greene's back porch. It sounded like paper being crumpled. I peered into the shadows until I caught a glimpse of that wild hair. I stopped far enough away so both Howie and I could stay brave. Besides, I needed a plan.

There was a walkway to the porch steps, but it was made from old bricks. Even if I didn't get stuck, I'd bump around a lot. The witch would hear me coming.

Howie put his lips right to my ear. "My tummy feels sick," he whispered.

I tried to smile at him. "Too much candy!" I whispered back.

Then the witch started down the steps. Without even thinking, I backed away a little. She was carrying something like a huge bowl with long legs. All I could think of was a cauldron. Then I remembered the matches. Was she going to start a *fire* in all that dry grass? She didn't notice us. She went the other way into the yard.

I heard Zelda bark, far away. Good. Maybe Just Rick was back with Tina.

Then I heard Tina's voice. "Rick! Rick? Ri-ick!"

Rick had to be out there in the yard somewhere. If he'd guessed what I'd guessed, I wasn't sure what he'd do.

I decided I had to do something first.

"Howie," I whispered. "Come with me."

SEVEN

I could feel Howie relax as I crossed the street to Steffie's.

I stopped outside the light that shone from Steffie's porch. I took Howie's arm and coaxed him around to face me. I held him by both shoulders. "Now, lion," I whispered, "remember how we get the wicked witch?"

"Melt her!" he said, and I swear he even grinned. The scene in which the witch melts is his absolute favorite.

"Right," I said. I pointed to Steffie's big

pile of hose. "So real quiet now, grab that spray nozzle and hand it to me."

He had to cross into the light, but I prayed the witch still had her back turned. Howie brought me the nozzle, and the hose uncoiled behind him.

"You're the bravest lion in the world," I said. He grinned. "Now there's the faucet, see? If you use both hands, I bet you're strong enough to turn it."

Howie stepped over the coils of hose, his tail bouncing behind him. He bent over the the faucet handle and tried to turn it. He stood up and looked back at me. "I can't, Mags," he said, and a little squeak came into his whisper.

I glanced over my shoulder.

The witch lit a match. It fizzled right out, but the next one might not.

"We have to melt her!" I whispered to Howie as loud as I dared.

When he tried again, there were a lot of gurgling and hissing sounds.

"Great!" I said. "Now turn it all the way."

I hooked the nozzle handle to my chair and held up both arms like a muscle man to Howie. He did the same and flashed a huge, whiskered smile. He was actually having fun.

"Now you wait here," I whispered. "Sit on Steffie's steps, okay?"

"Hey, no fair!" he said, almost forgetting to whisper.

I figured if this was all a game to him, he might as well be part of the action.

"Okay," I said.

When I wheeled back across the lane, Howie made a big display of crouching and tiptoeing behind me. I almost felt like laughing. The hose uncoiled to follow us, and I was glad there weren't any cars coming. I wasn't sure how far the spray would reach, so I even pushed a little into the grass. I couldn't see the witch, but I could hear her trying to light another match.

Then Zelda barked nearby. Another match flared, and I saw Just Rick facing the witch. He looked so scared and angry, *he* was spooky.

The witch lit a small piece of paper and lowered it toward the bowl. No, it wasn't a bowl. It was one of those old charcoal grills. We had one before we got the gas kind. GAS! What if . . . ?

Before I even knew what I was thinking, I squeezed the spray nozzle and blasted that fire.

"Hey," Howie said, tugging at the hose. "*I* want to melt her!"

"What the . . ." the witch burst out.

She forgot to disguise her voice, and suddenly I realized I *knew* that witch. The flame had gone out right away, but I kept whipping that water around to make sure I hit my target.

"No fair," Howie was whining, but I wouldn't give him the nozzle. The witch came stumbling toward me, both hands held up for protection. I aimed for the mask.

"Hey!" came Mark Lowman's voice. He tripped and fell.

"She's melting!" Howie yelled. "She's melting!"

Mark rolled over facedown, but I kept right

on spraying. I couldn't believe he'd go to all
that trouble just to be a jerk. How did he even
know where I lived? We weren't even in the
phone book yet. I was mad at him for scaring
Howie. I was mad at him for scaring Just
Rick. And I felt like I could *kill* him for scaring *me*!

"She's melting!" Howie kept yelling.
Now I locked the nozzle full on and let him
have a turn.

Zelda circled the writhing witch, barking
furiously. Then we heard sirens. Just Rick
came toward us out of the darkness. Tina
came running around the corner. The sirens
came closer and a fire truck went by up
Greene Street. Another turned into the lane
and stopped short with its huge lights flashing.
Howie turned toward it with his mouth wide
open, forgetting about the nozzle in his hand.
I had to grab it back to keep him from spraying me.

EIGHT

It felt like maybe two seconds before a crowd had gathered. Steffie was there, and the neighbors from up the lane. A lot of trick-or-treaters appeared, too, including the box of Cheerios. Everyone was talking at once and asking questions no one could answer. Several lights went on in the big house. Voices crackled over the fire truck's radio. Firefighters had spread out among us. The chief came up to me.

That's when I realized I was still spraying

Mark Lowman. I let go of the trigger and dropped the nozzle. A firefighter bent over Mark.

The chief stuck out his hand to shake mine. "Maggie Mitzkovitz, if I remember correctly."

I shook his hand. "Hi, Mr. Gibb," I said. We'd met that time there were false alarms at school.

Mr. Gibb stood back and folded his arms across his chest. "You the one pulled the alarm?"

"No, sir, I did." It was Just Rick. "I thought . . ." he said, but then looked down. "Sorry, sir. I guess we didn't need—"

"Well, actually," I started, but then Mark Lowman groaned and sat up.

Mr. Gibb turned to look at the soggy heap. "Now let me guess," he said. "She—"

"He—" I corrected.

"Was lighting fires," Just Rick finished.

"So," Howie said. He tugged on Mr. Gibb's sleeve. "We melted the witch!"

Mr. Gibb walked over to Mark. "Take off the mask," he said.

Mark tried to look around at all the people, but the mask had gotten all twisted. The eye-holes were on the side of his head.

"Now!" Mr. Gibb said.

Mark took off the mask. His hair stuck out in crazy, wet spikes. There were little titters from the crowd. He looked like an alien or something.

I took Howie by the hand. "See," I said. "It's just a kid. There's no such thing as a real witch." I didn't have to mention how spooked I'd been myself.

Then a big commotion erupted behind me.

"Please let us through," I heard Dad say. "Please let us through."

"Excuse us," Mom was saying. "Howie? Maggie?"

"We're okay, Mom," I called, twisting in my chair to greet her.

She burst through the crowd and bent to grab both Howie and me in a crushing hug. Dad came around in front of me and hugged us, too. The crowd got all quiet for a second.

As soon as Mom and Dad stood up, the questions started buzzing around again.

"And you, I presume," said Mr. Gibb to Mom and Dad, "are the parents of this fine young lady?"

"Jane May," Mom said, extending her hand. That's when I realized she was still all covered with blue dots.

Mr. Gibb cleared his throat carefully. "I can see the family resemblance," he said.

"Bob Mitzkovitz," Dad said. "What's going on?"

"I'd love to know that myself," said Mr. Gibb.

"We melted the wicked witch!" Howie explained.

"Mark was lighting matches," I said, "and—"

"I pulled the alarm," Just Rick said. "Over on Greene Street."

Tina spoke up now. "And then Rick went after her—uh, him—again. I tried to stop him, but—"

"I have to tell you," I interrupted. "I think I might have smelled gas."

Dad chuckled and took off my funnel. "Remember?" he said.

"No, I mean *gas* gas. Like from the stove."

That's when Mr. Gibb got all serious again. "Helen," he called to one of the firefighters, "call in the gas company, will you?"

"I don't smell anything," she said.

"Believe me," Mr. Gibb answered. "We can trust this girl's nose."

"But maybe not," I said. "There's this disguise—"

"Doesn't cover your nose," Mr. Gibb said as he turned away.

"But it does mask . . ."

I didn't bother to finish. Mr. Gibb wasn't paying attention to me. He was telling the firefighters to spread out through the tall grass. They swung their flashlight beams from side to side and sniffed the air.

I was going to feel pretty dumb if the gas

company showed up and told me all I'd smelled was chrysanthemums.

The woman firefighter came back with the grill. She set it down and shone her flashlight into it. On top of the heap of soggy newspaper was a small piece of lined paper. It was charred at the edges, but I could still see writing that looked familiar. I picked it up. Some of it was still readable: "Need a scarecrow? . . . Be there."

Just Rick stared at it, too. Our note. I'd written down my address and the time we were going out. But how had Mark gotten it? Then I remembered Mark picking up trash from the floor. I'd even thought he was being *nice*. Yeah, right!

I felt like spraying him again, but Mr. Gibb was standing over him.

"Get up, young man," Mr. Gibb said.

Mark stood up. I think he was trying to look cocky, but he was shivering too hard.

Mr. Gibb faced him squarely. "What's your name, young man?"

"Mark."

"Mark what?"

"Lowman."

"Have you got anything to say for yourself?"

"I was just having a little fun," Mark said. He spoke in a rush between attacks of the shivers. "Just 'cause that kid's such a scaredy-cat—"

Mark was gesturing at Rick, but Mr. Gibb glanced at Howie. "So terrifying little kids is your idea of fun?"

"I meant . . ." Mark was having trouble holding his head up. "Anyway, I was being safe."

"Safe, young man?" Mr. Gibb kicked at the trampled grass. "In this tinder box? You're lucky this young lady here has a good head on her shoulders."

I noticed my stomach still felt uneasy. I wished Mr. Gibb hadn't mentioned me. The only thanks I'd get would be more trouble from Mark.

"Do you realize," Mr. Gibb said to Mark,

"that an elderly woman lives in that house?" He pointed up at Mrs. Greene's towers.

Mark didn't answer. He put his arms around himself and shivered some more. He looked like he wished he really could melt away.

Mr. Gibb didn't let up. "If there'd been a fire, she'd be *trapped* in there."

As if on cue, a light went on on the back porch of the big house.

NINE

Everyone's attention turned.

The gas company workers were arriving and a firefighter went to talk to them, but no one took much notice. We were all looking up at Mrs. Greene's back porch.

It took a minute before the door opened. I was startled. The woman who came out was no older than Mom. But then I realized she was wearing a nurse's uniform and pushing a wheelchair in front of her. A wheelchair? Mrs. Greene used a wheelchair? Then where were the ramps?

The nurse positioned the wheelchair at the top of the steps. In the bright light of the porch Mrs. Greene's hair looked whiter than white. Her face was almost as pale, except when the red light from the firetruck swung across it. Her shoulders were bent and covered with a shawl, but she held her head up. Her eyes were dark and sharp.

"Whatever is going on here?" she asked. Her voice was thin, but not the least bit shaky.

"Hello, Emma," said Mr. Gibb. "Sorry to disturb you. Just some Halloween foolishness, I think. No cause for alarm. We'll—"

That's when one of the gas workers came running up. "Could I talk to you, Chief?"

Now we all noticed the other worker, poking all over the yard with a big, orange, stick-like probe.

The whole crowd went silent, trying to hear what was whispered to Mr. Gibb. We didn't have to wait long to know.

Mr. Gibb turned to us all. "I want complete quiet," he said, "and complete calm."

The complete quiet he got, but everyone

was tense to bursting. "We've detected some gas fumes," he said. "We need to clear the area."

Everyone started shuffling around and talking.

"SILENCE," Mr. Gibb commanded. He reminded me of Mr. Buckley. "If you don't live here or in that house," he said, pointing at Steffie's across the lane, "then please go home."

The edges of the crowd began dispersing. Mark Lowman turned to leave.

"You stay here," Mr. Gibb said. "Helen, could you get this young man a blanket from the truck?" The chief raised his voice again. "And if you *do* live across the way there, please go home with someone else. This shouldn't take long."

He turned to look up at Mrs. Greene. "I'm sorry, Emma, but we'll have to evacuate you for a while. We can carry you in that chair right down these stairs."

"She shouldn't be out in this cold," the nurse said.

"Nonsense," Mrs. Greene said. "I've had a stroke, not pneumonia." She straightened the blanket over her lap.

Dad went up with some other people to help carry her down. "I'm experienced at this," he said.

Mrs. Greene sat up very straight.

"Like a queen on her palanquin," Dad said as they set her down.

I looked at Just Rick. He was smiling.

"Oh come on," I said. "Don't tell me you know what *that* meant! Pallinkeen?"

"Just guessing," Rick said. "But I bet it's a throne—like maybe that kind people carry."

Mom had gone up to introduce herself to Mrs. Greene. "You're welcome to come to our house," Mom said.

Mrs. Greene glanced at my wheelchair and smiled. "I'd be delighted," she said.

"And you, too, Steffie," Dad added. "Come on, Howie. Come on, Maggie."

"But Daddy!" Howie protested loudly. He held up three fingers again. "We still get three more treats!"

Everyone laughed except Steffie. "How about I give you my leftovers?" she said.

"I thought you ran out," Howie said.

Steffie shook her head. "*Lots* left."

"I'll have courage forever!" Howie crowed.

Mr. Gibb went up to Mom and Dad. "Mind harboring the criminal till I have a minute?"

"No problem," Dad said. "I'll find him some dry clothes."

That's how Mark Lowman ended up at my house for a party—because it did turn out to be a party. Mom put Howie to bed and Dad made cocoa, and there we all were, crowded into our living room: Steffie and Mrs. Greene and the nurse, who turned out to be Ms. Fuente; Tina and Just Rick and Zelda; my parents and me.

At first, Mark slouched in the corner, wearing a sweatsuit of Dad's that wasn't all that big on him.

The first thing I'd done was give that funnel back to Dad and scrub off every trace of my greasepaint. I sat there not drinking my cocoa because I was just enjoying the unmasked smell.

Mrs. Greene seemed to think this was the biggest social event of the decade. Maybe for her it was. Her cheeks were turning pink. She bragged about her age—ninety-six. It turned out she'd just gotten out of the hospital after a stroke. The wheelchair was new.

''So now you need a ramp over there,'' Dad said.

Dad was a builder till he came here to go to business school. I knew where his conversation was going.

I watched Mrs. Greene talking to Dad. I felt extremely dumb. I had to admit that I'd thought she might be the witch—just because she was old and lived in an old house. Assuming old ladies are hags isn't all that different from assuming wheelchair users are pathetic.

When I listened again to the conversation, Mrs. Greene was thanking Dad for the ramps he was going to build.

Then the doorbell rang.

We figured it was late trick-or-treaters. Mom opened the door with the bowl of candy in her hand.

"No thanks," said Mr. Gibb, smiling.

I guess we'd almost forgotten about the danger.

Mr. Gibb wiped his feet carefully before he stepped into the room. "Well, they found a gas leak, all right. Right by your back porch, Emma. Old line got turned off at the house, but not at the supply end. I'm surprised no one felt sick."

"But I *did*," I said, "and so did Howie."

"Me, too," Mark mumbled from his corner.

Mr. Gibb looked Mark straight in the eye. "Mighty lucky that fire never got going."

"I'm so grateful to you," Mrs. Greene told Mr. Gibb.

"Don't thank *me*," he said. He gestured at me. "Thank Maggie, our olfactory wizard!"

I didn't have to ask Rick about *olfactory*. Since it refers to the sense of smell, I've heard it a million times.

But I noticed Rick's shoulders were shaking. Then came the muffled snorting.

"Okay," I said, "so what's so funny this time?"

Everyone looked at him.

He could barely get the words out. "The chief just—" More snorting laughter. Everybody smiled just watching him. "What I mean is," he finally spluttered, "the chief just called Maggie the Wizard of Schnoz!"

Everyone roared with laughter, Mr. Gibb included.

It took me a second.

"Schnoz," Dad said, still gasping. "Big nose!"

As I joined the laughter, I noticed even Mark was grinning.

TEN

In school the next morning, everybody looked tired—Jo especially. Mark Lowman wasn't even there.

"Hi, Maggie," Jo said. "What'd you do last night?"

Debby answered for me. "She was the tin man, remember?"

"Oh yeah. And Herbie was the cowardly lion, right?"

"Howie," I said. "And it turns out he's very brave." I smiled, just thinking about

74

Howie helping me melt the witch. "How was your party?" I asked.

Jo shrugged. "Okay, I guess."

Debby looked at her. "Come on, Jo. It was not."

I was amazed. Deb's usually like Jo's shadow, always agreeing with her. Maybe even Deb had some hidden courage.

The bell rang as Deb started to tell me about the party. "We got in serious tr—"

"Okay, attendance!" Mr. Buckley announced. "Take your seats."

For me that meant wheeling into place at my table. Just Rick was already there, and Tina came and sat with us.

After the attendance and the lunch count, Mr. Buckley put us right to work. It was Friday, which meant writing in our journals. I wanted to write about what had happened. The problem was, Mr. Buckley reads our journals. That would feel like tattling on Mark. I didn't know why I cared, but I kept seeing the look on his face as he watched the rest of us having a good time in my living room. I thought maybe I could tell the story leaving Mark out, but how could I admit what a jerk *I* had been about Mrs. Greene?

I looked across at Tina and Just Rick. They were both scribbling madly. I was pretty sure *they* wouldn't tell on Mark either. Tina looked up at me and smiled.

"I have two great friends," I wrote in my journal.

Then the classroom door opened and Mark Lowman walked in. He was acting like his old self: cocky. He did glance sideways at my table, though. Did the tiniest hint of a grin cross his face? I wasn't sure.

"You'll have to go down to the office," Mr. Buckley told him. "I've already marked you absent."

While Mark was gone, his buddies at the next table were whispering. Mark had probably bragged about his plans. Now his friends were waiting for a good story. I wondered what he'd tell them.

I went back to my journal. I got to thinking about Tina leaving that party and Just Rick facing fires, and Howie following me around that corner. I was wondering if maybe there was a little courage in everybody, when Mark Lowman strode back into class.

Then the weirdest thing happened. Mark walked over to our table, pulled out an empty chair, and sat down—right across from me. He paid very close attention to getting a pencil from his backpack.

The whole room was completely silent for a second. Then everyone seemed to shift position.

At the first whispers, Mr. Buckley cleared his throat. "This work needs no discussion," he announced firmly. I swear there was a smile in his voice.

I tried to catch Mark's eye, but he kept his head bent as if journal writing was his favorite thing. I turned to a blank page in my notebook and drew a big medal with ribbons and all. BADGE OF COURAGE, I wrote across the middle. It took me a long time to tear the page out without Mr. Buckley noticing, but then I folded the thing a million times and pushed it across the table to Mark. He jammed it into his back pocket without even looking at it.

A little while later, Mark excused himself to go to the bathroom. When he came back, he dropped the note in front of me. It was still folded. He hadn't even looked at it. I had to admit, I was a little disappointed. Mr. Buckley was strolling around, so I quickly put the note in my sweatshirt pocket.

"So, what was in the note?" Tina asked at recess.

I took it out and unfolded it to show her the badge of courage. Then I noticed something scribbled at the bottom. Mark had written, "Same to you."

I looked around the playground. Mark was back with his buddies.

"What do you think he told them?" Tina said.

I smiled. "Something that makes him a hero."

Just Rick shrugged. "Probably."

"But I bet he won't bug us anymore," I said.

Just Rick smiled and looked at his feet. He shuffled them a few times. I could tell there was something on his mind.

"So," he said.

"Yeah?" I coaxed.

He looked over his shoulder as if someone might be eavesdropping. "So we could celebrate," he said to his feet.

"Yeah, let's!" Tina said.

"I mean ..." Shuffle, shuffle. "Tomorrow's my birthday."

"Hey! Happy Birthday!" Tina and I both said.

Rick smiled without looking at us. "Well, I wasn't going to have a party or anything, but now, I mean, if you both came to my house ..."

Tina glanced at me.

Now I stared at *my* feet. I'd thought Just Rick understood. Going to other people's houses is something I can't do. Why should I have to keep pointing that out?

"Maggie?" Rick said.

He kind of dipped his head to catch my eye. There was just the slightest grin on his face. It confused me.

"Listen," I started.

"No excuses," he said. "My house, Saturday, two to four."

He was definitely grinning now, and it reminded me of how much looser he'd been out of school. Something was cracking him up.

"I don't get it," I said, smiling without wanting to.

"Oh, maybe I didn't tell you!"

"Tell me what?"

"We bought our house from an old guy. He was moving to a nursing home."

"So?" I said.

Tina caught on before I did. "Old like Mrs. Greene, you mean?"

"Yeah."

They both stood there grinning at me till the light dawned: The old man had used a wheelchair. Just Rick lived in a house with ramps.

"You're kidding," I said.

Just Rick shrugged. "Why would I?"

I wanted to shout. I sort of wanted to cry. A friend who could invite me over!

The bell rang, and as I turned my chair toward our classroom, Tina and Just Rick got on either side and linked elbows with me. I rolled along easily between them.

"I don't believe it!" I kept saying. "I don't believe it!"

Mark Lowman and his buddies looked over at us. His buddies grinned and glanced at him. They were waiting for him to say something they could laugh at. But I recognized the look on Mark's face. It was the one I'd seen in my living room—a little sad and a little left out. I guess he'd noticed what I was noticing: I'm a pretty lucky kid.

THE MAGIC CONTINUES...
WITH
LYNNE REID BANKS

THE INDIAN IN THE CUPBOARD
60012-9/$4.50 US/$6.50 Can

THE RETURN OF THE INDIAN
70284-3/$3.99 US

THE SECRET OF THE INDIAN
71040-4/$4.50 US

THE MYSTERY OF THE CUPBOARD
72013-2/$4.50 US/$6.50 Can

I, HOUDINI
70649-0/$4.50 US

THE FAIRY REBEL
70650-4/$4.50 US

THE FARTHEST-AWAY MOUNTAIN
71303-9/$4.50 US

ONE MORE RIVER
71563-5/$3.99 US

THE ADVENTURES OF KING MIDAS
71564-3/$4.50 US

THE MAGIC HARE
71562-7/$5.99 US

MAKE TODAY YOUR ~~UN~~LUCKY DAY!
READ ALL 13
SPINETINGLERS BY
M. T. COFFIN

#1	**The Substitute Creature**	77829-7/$3.50US/$4.50Can
#2	**Billy Baker's Dog Won't Stay Buried**	
		77742-8/$3.50US/$4.50Can
#3	**My Teacher's a Bug**	77785-1/$3.50US/$4.50Can
#4	**Where Have All the Parents Gone?**	
		78117-4/$3.50US/$4.50Can
#5	**Check It Out—and Die!**	78116-6/$3.50US/$4.50Can
#6	**Simon Says, "Croak!"**	78232-4/$3.50US/$4.50Can
#7	**Snow Day**	78157-3/$3.50US/$4.50Can
#8	**Don't Go to the Principal's Office**	
		78313-4/$3.50US/$4.99Can
#9	**Step on a Crack**	78432-7/$3.50US/$4.99Can
#10	**The Dead Kid Did It**	78314-2/$3.50US/$4.99Can
#11	**Fly by Night**	78366-5/$3.50US/$4.99Can
#12	**Killer Computer**	78312-6/$3.50US/$4.99Can
#13	**Pet Store**	78460-2/$3.50US/$4.99Can